Knights of the Round Table

adapted by
Gwen Gross

illustrated by
Norman Green

cover illustrated by
Corey Wolfe

A STEPPING STONE BOOK™

Random House 🏠 New York

Text copyright © 1985 by Random House, Inc. Illustrations copyright © 1985
by Norman Green. Cover illustration copyright © 2004 by Corey Wolfe. All rights
reserved under International and Pan-American Copyright Conventions. Published in
the United States by Random House Children's Books, a division of Random House,
Inc., New York, and simultaneously in Canada by Random House of Canada Limited,
Toronto. Originally published in a slightly different form by Random House, Inc.,
in 1985.

www.randomhouse.com/kids

Library of Congress Cataloging-in-Publication Data
Gross, Gwen.
Knights of the Round Table / adapted by Gwen Gross ; illustrated by Norman Green.
   p. cm. — "A stepping stone book."
SUMMARY: Retells the exploits of King Arthur and his knights of the Round Table.
ISBN 0-394-87579-6 (trade) — ISBN 0-394-97579-0 (lib. bdg.)
1. Arthurian romances—Adaptations. [1. Arthur, King—Legends. 2. Knights and
knighthood—Folklore. 3. Folklore—England.] I. Green, Norman, 1934– , ill. II. Title.
PZ8.1.G858Kn 2004 398.2'0942'02—dc22 2003023531

Printed in the United States of America :   50 49 48

Contents

Contents

Preface

There are many tales of a wonderful king named Arthur. And of the brave knights of the Round Table.

Who told the first story of King Arthur? No one knows. The tales are very old. They have been told by many different storytellers in many different lands. And each told the stories in his own special way.

Was there a real King Arthur? People who study the past think there was. They know only a little about him. He ruled in England about fifteen hundred years ago. He won many battles. And he was a king no one could forget.

· 1 ·

The Sword in the Stone

It was a cold, windy night. The moon shone on a huge stone castle built high on a hill. It was the castle of King Uther of England.

All at once a strange shining mist began to move and swirl near the castle gate. Then the mist was gone. In its place stood an old man. He wore a dark robe and a tall pointed hat. He had a long white beard. And strange silvery eyes.

The old man looked toward the castle. The gate opened and two women came out. One carried a tiny baby wrapped in a golden cloth.

The old man held out his arms. Without a word, the woman gave him the baby. The shining mist came again. When it cleared, the old man and the baby had vanished.

Where had they gone?

Deep in a forest many miles away stood a smaller castle. It belonged to a knight called Sir Ector. He was known for his goodness and honesty.

Sir Ector was climbing the stone steps to his room. But a golden mist surrounded him. And then a strange old man was there. He had a baby in his arms.

"Merlin!" Ector cried. Ector knew the old man well. He was Merlin. The master of magic. The most powerful wizard in the world. Ector feared Merlin. But he trusted him too. Merlin used his powers for good.

"Why do you come here?" Ector asked.

Merlin held out the baby. "I bring you this child. I ask you to raise him as your own son. I cannot tell you why. Name him Arthur. And tell no one how he came to you."

Gently Ector took the baby. "I will do all that you ask," he said.

In an instant Merlin had disappeared. But Ector could still hear him whisper, *"Tell no one."*

Ector looked down at the baby. "All will be well, Arthur. I will love you just as I love my own son, Kay," he told him. Then he frowned. "But who are you? What is your secret?"

Sixteen years passed. Arthur became a strong, handsome boy. He was studying to be a knight like his older brother, Sir Kay.

Arthur had learned to ride. To shoot a bow and arrow. To fight with sword and spear and dagger. He knew too that a knight had to be brave and kind and honest. He felt ready for adventure. But nothing ever happened at the castle.

Then one winter day a stranger rode up to the castle. Arthur was out hunting. But Sir Ector and Sir Kay welcomed the stranger. The man came from London. He looked tired. But his face was full of excitement. He told a strange and wonderful tale.

"Since King Uther died, many knights and lords have fought to wear the crown," the stranger began.

"I feared the fighting would never end. But on Christmas Day a miracle happened! Rich and poor were crowded into the Great Church. They

spilled into the churchyard. I was among them.

"Suddenly there was a blinding light. A great white stone appeared in the yard. No one knows how. It stood where nothing had been just an instant before. A shining sword rose out of the stone. On it were these words:

"WHOEVER CAN DRAW THIS SWORD
FROM THIS STONE
IS THE TRUE KING OF ENGLAND."

"Could anyone do it?" Sir Ector asked.

"No one has tried yet," the stranger said. "But on New Year's Day there will be a tournament. Knights and lords will come from far and wide. They will show their skill with sword and spear. Afterward anyone who wishes to be king can try to draw the sword from the stone."

Sir Kay's eyes were sparkling. "A tournament! Can we go, Father?"

Sir Ector smiled. "We will leave at once for London. Find Arthur."

Sir Kay ran out. Arthur was coming from the stable. "Arthur!" he cried. "We are going to London! I am to fight in a tournament. We must make ready!"

London! Arthur was even more excited than Kay. Beyond the castle was the chance for adventure. There were strange beasts. Robbers. Wicked knights. Fairies and wizards. Anything might happen!

They set out. They traveled all day. And they slept under the stars that night. The next morning they had not gone far when Arthur saw something in the distance. A great wall. Towers and more towers jutting into the sky. London!

Arthur rode into the city with Sir Ector and Sir Kay. There were so many buildings and shops and churches. And so many people. Rich ladies. Beggars in rags. Shopkeepers selling their goods. Lords on horseback. Arthur had never seen such sights. He wanted to look everywhere at once.

Finally they stopped at an inn. But only long enough to rest their horses. It was New Year's Day. The tournament was to begin soon. They did not want to be late.

The playing field was near the Great Church. Flags were flying. There were tents of bright-colored silk. Beautiful horses prancing. Knights in gleaming armor. It was wonderful!

Then Kay cried, "Oh, no!"

"What is wrong?" Arthur asked.

Kay looked miserable. "The tournament is about to begin. And I left my sword at the inn."

Arthur was always quick to help. "Do not worry," he said. "I will go back and fetch it for you."

Arthur galloped away from the playing field. But when he reached the inn, it was closed. When he knocked, no one answered. Everyone was at the tournament.

Arthur did not want his brother to miss it. But what could he do? Arthur started back to the tournament. As he rode past the Great Church he noticed something in the churchyard. A sword stuck in a big white stone.

Perhaps that sword would do for Kay!

Arthur jumped from his horse. He ran to the stone. No one else was there. Arthur grasped the sword. He pulled it out easily.

Then he rode back to Kay. "I could not bring your sword," he told him. "But this one will do as well."

Kay frowned. "Where did you find it?" he asked.

"It was in a stone in the old churchyard," Arthur answered.

Kay turned pale. The sword in the stone!

"Wait here," Kay said to Arthur. Then he snatched the sword from Arthur and went to Sir Ector.

"Father, look!" Kay cried. "I must be the King of England! I have the magic sword!"

Sir Ector looked at his son. He didn't speak for a long moment. Then, very quietly, he said, "How do you come to have this sword?"

Kay blushed. He couldn't meet his father's eyes. Finally he said, "Arthur brought the sword to me."

Sir Ector stood. "We must get Arthur."

Sir Ector, Sir Kay, and Arthur went quickly to the churchyard. They reached the stone.

"Arthur," Sir Ector said, "how did you come to have this sword?"

Arthur was worried. He hadn't meant to do anything wrong. "I wanted to help Kay," he said. "He needed a sword. I took it from this stone."

"Arthur," Sir Ector said, "put the sword back into the stone."

Arthur was puzzled. But he did as he was told.

"Now, Kay," Sir Ector told his son, "pull it out."

Kay held the sword. He pulled and pulled. Nothing happened.

Sir Ector grasped the sword himself. It did not move.

"Now you, Arthur," Ector said.

Arthur stepped up to the stone. He pulled out the sword. Just as he had before.

Sir Ector went down on his knees. "I bow to the true King of England," he said. Kay kneeled beside him.

"Father, what do you mean?" Arthur cried.

Sir Ector looked up at him. "I have loved you like my own child. But you are not my son. Merlin the wizard brought you to me. You were only a baby. I promised to raise you. And to keep the secret."

Arthur could not believe his ears. His father not his father? He was to be king? He felt afraid and excited and lonely all at once.

"Please rise, Father," Arthur told Sir Ector. "I must know what to do. I am afraid."

Sir Ector put his hand on Arthur's shoulder. "Let us go back to the tournament. Afterward we will come here with the others. You must draw out the sword again. Before them all."

Later that day the churchyard was crowded. The proud knights and lords who hoped to draw the sword from the stone were there. And people had come from miles around to watch them try. They all wished a great knight would become king that day.

Arthur was in the crowd too. He watched the knights. One by one they walked boldly to the stone and tried to pull out the sword. But no one could.

"Go, Arthur," Sir Ector whispered. "Go to the stone."

But Arthur would not. He felt afraid. What if he failed now?

Finally the last knight had had his turn. The people in the churchyard sighed with disappointment. Some began to turn and leave.

Arthur knew he must try. Slowly he moved through the crowd. He still wore his everyday clothes. He looked young and shy. People began to frown and stare. He heard their whispers.

"Who is that?" they asked. "He looks like an ordinary boy." And then there were louder voices. "Does he dare to touch the sword?"

Arthur tried not to listen. He kept walking. He had almost reached the stone. He stopped. The stone looked much bigger now. The sword more beautiful. He felt everyone's eyes on him. They were waiting. He took a step forward. He grasped the sword. He took one great breath and pulled. The sword seemed to tremble in his hand. Then out it came!

For a moment no one made a sound. Then someone called, "That boy cannot be the king! It must be a trick. He is not even a knight!"

Arthur just stood there. He did not know what to do or say.

Suddenly a bright golden mist swirled through the churchyard. And a strange old man was there. It was Merlin!

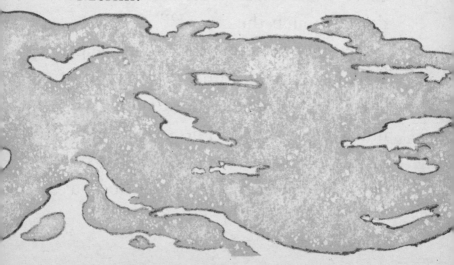

"The great wizard!" the people whispered. Then they were quiet.

Merlin smiled kindly at Arthur. And somehow Arthur felt he had known this old man all his life.

Merlin turned to the crowd. "I have a tale of wonder to tell!" he cried. "For I know the past. And I know the future. Before King Uther died, he had a son. He named him Arthur. The king's enemies wanted to kill his baby. I hid him away where no one would harm him. Now his time has come. He will take the throne. And he will be the greatest king that England has ever known. King Arthur!"

There was silence. Then a great roar filled the churchyard. "The king! We have found our king!"

Arthur was no longer afraid. And he knew that what the wizard said was true. He was meant to be king.

Arthur looked at the faces in the crowd. He saw people of all ages. Some wore jewels and fine clothes. Some looked poor and tired. They were all staring at him. Hope was shining in their eyes. He wanted to speak to them.

"I will be your king," he said. "I will fight the powers of evil. And I will try to bring peace and justice for all."

He kneeled. Merlin came forward. He placed the crown on Arthur's head. The crowd began to cheer again. "Long live King Arthur!"

· 2 ·

Lancelot and the Round Table

Church bells were ringing! Crowds were cheering!

It was King Arthur's wedding day. He was coming to his castle in the city of Camelot. His beautiful new bride was with him.

"Look! Look!" someone cried. Down the street came a great parade of knights and ladies. All on fine horses and wearing their brightest jewels. Last of all came King Arthur with Queen Guinevere. The loveliest lady in all the wide world.

Inside the castle Merlin greeted everyone. Then he led King Arthur and his knights to the Great Hall. He bowed to Arthur. "This is a great day of joy!" he said. "It will mark the beginning of our kingdom's greatest glory. Stand back!"

Merlin lifted his hand. Suddenly a huge round table stood in the Great Hall. It was made of stone and wood. Around it were many, many chairs. One hundred and fifty of them!

Merlin's voice rang out. "We are at a great dawning. At this Round Table will sit the bravest knights in the world. And they will be brothers. They will travel through the land. They will fight for what is right and good. Many will die. But the fame of the knights of the Round Table will live on. Forever."

Arthur stood. "My noble knights, let us promise together. We will fight only for what is fair and good. Never for riches. Never for a selfish cause. We will help all those who ask for help. We will stand by one another. We will be gentle to the weak. But terrible to the wicked."

"We promise!" the knights said in one voice.

Merlin spoke again. "And here are your places." On every chair gold letters appeared. They spelled the name of the knight who was to sit there.

When all the knights were seated, only a few places were empty. Arthur looked around the table. He was proud of the men he saw. There was his brother, Sir Kay. And Sir Ector. There was Sir Gawain, who always tried to do right. No matter what it cost him. Sir Bedivere, Sir Lamorack, and so many more.

"What fine, fine men they are!" Arthur said to Merlin.

Merlin answered in a voice everyone could hear. "Indeed they are. But the greatest knight of all is still to come. He will be like the leopard and the lamb."

Then a golden mist appeared. And Merlin was gone.

Sir Kay joked, "Am *I* not the greatest?" And the knights laughed. Kay had little skill with the sword.

Just then a servant whispered to Arthur, "A stranger wishes to see you."

"Let him come," said Arthur.

Soon a young man stood before the Round Table. He was tall and strong. He was not handsome. Yet there was something about his face. It was hard to look away from him.

"My name is Lancelot," the young

man said. "I come from a land across the sea. I wish to become a knight. I will try in all ways to bring honor to you."

The young man waited for King Arthur's answer. He stood very, very still.

King Arthur looked closely at Lancelot. There was great power and courage in his face. But great kindness, too. His eyes were the gentlest that King Arthur had ever seen. He remembered Merlin's words—the leopard and the lamb. "Yes," he thought, "Lancelot looks as fierce as a leopard. And as gentle as a lamb. He must be the knight of whom Merlin spoke. The greatest knight of all."

King Arthur said, "Please kneel." He drew his sword and touched it to

the young man's shoulder. "Rise, Sir
Lancelot." Then he pointed to the seat
next to his. "This will be your place."
And it seemed to him that even before
he spoke, gold letters appeared on the
chair. They spelled LANCELOT.

Sir Lancelot sat down slowly. He could not help but hear voices muttering, "What do we know of this boy? Why should he sit beside the king?"

And then the knights began to call, "Sir Lancelot! May we ask what brave deeds you have done?"

Sir Lancelot's face turned red. "None," he said quietly.

There was a surprised silence.

Sir Lancelot stared down at the table. Then he stood. He cleared his throat. "I have a place at this table. But I have not earned it. I will go now and try to prove that I deserve to sit among you. In a year and a day I will return. And then I hope you will welcome me."

Sir Lancelot rode away from the castle. He had just reached the forest when he saw a very strange sight.

A knight on horseback had stopped on the path. Suddenly he cried out. He fell back just as though he had been hit. But no one else was there. Sir Lancelot heard the sound of hoof-beats growing louder. He felt as though someone was galloping right past him. He heard an evil laugh. But still he saw no one!

The fallen knight was moaning. Sir Lancelot hurried to him. "Let me help you," he said.

"Beware!" the knight cried. "Sir Garlon is about! He is very wicked. And he can make himself invisible! I am not badly hurt. But Sir Garlon will be back. He will kill us both."

Sir Lancelot jumped on his horse. How could he fight someone he could not see?

All at once he heard hoofbeats again.

And the same evil laugh. Sir Garlon was almost upon him. Sir Lancelot had to do something.

With one hand he threw off his cloak. Would it land on Sir Garlon? Yes! It clung to the knight. Now Sir Lancelot could see his shape clearly. He aimed his spear and drove it in. There was a cry and a crash. Then a knight in armor began to appear. Stretched out on the ground!

"You have beaten Sir Garlon!" the other knight cried.

Sir Lancelot told him to tie up Sir Garlon and take him to King Arthur.

"I will," the knight answered. "And I thank you. You are the greatest knight I have ever seen!"

Sir Lancelot did not hear him. He was already on his way.

Sir Lancelot rode through the land. He rescued maidens from wicked knights. He fought for the weak and the poor. He never lost a battle.

One day Sir Lancelot was riding through beautiful green meadows and fields. Then all of a sudden the land changed. There were only charred trees. And grass burned black. Had a great fire come this way?

Sir Lancelot saw a huge white tower on a hill. Below it was a town. He thought he would learn the answer there. But as he drew closer he saw that the town was ruined and empty. The smell of ashes filled the air.

Then a man and a boy ran out from behind a blackened wall. "It's Sir Lancelot! At last you have come. Our prayers are answered."

Sir Lancelot stopped.

"Our town has been cursed!" the man cried. "But Merlin says we can be saved. By the best knight in the world. Surely that is you."

"I am no better than many a knight. But I will try to help you," said Sir Lancelot. "What is wrong?"

"Just go to the tower on the hill. I dare not tell you more." The man took the boy's hand and they ran off.

Why were they so afraid?

Sir Lancelot rode halfway up the

hill. He stopped and waited. At the bottom of the tower was a huge door. It was open. But Lancelot could not see inside. He heard a kind of low hissing. Then he saw the most terrible sight of his life. Green scaly skin. Huge claws. Sharp pointed teeth and a mouth that spit fire! It was a dragon. A huge dragon!

The dragon moved through the door. It stared at Sir Lancelot with evil eyes. It gave a great roar and ran toward him.

Sir Lancelot galloped straight at it. He aimed his spear. It flew through the air and landed in the dragon's throat! Flames burst from the monster's mouth. Clouds of poison filled the air. The dragon was badly hurt. But it kept coming at Sir Lancelot. Lancelot leaped from his horse and drew his sword. He slashed at the dragon again and again. His armor was burning hot. He could hardly see. He was growing weak. He sank to his knees. With all the strength left in him he lifted his sword. In it went, deep into the dragon's heart. The monster shook. It blasted the air with fire and smoke. And then it died.

The man and the boy ran up the hill. Crowds of people followed them. "Sir Lancelot!" they called. "God bless you!"

They gave him food and drink. The man said, "For three years the dragon tormented us. It burned our homes

and fields. It killed our children. We hid in the forest. We dared not return. But you have saved us."

The townspeople begged Sir Lancelot to stay with them and rest. But he rode on. He fought a band of fifty thieves! He killed two evil giants! No danger was too great for him.

At last it was time to return to Camelot. To join the Round Table. Sir Lancelot wondered what welcome he would find there.

The castle was dark when Sir Lancelot reached it. He was glad. "Everyone must be asleep," he thought. He would find a corner to rest in. And the next day he could quietly take his place at the Round Table. He opened the door to the Great Hall. Suddenly it was bright with torches and candles. Everyone was there. King Arthur. Queen Guinevere. Merlin. All the knights and their ladies. They were clapping and smiling and calling his name! They had been waiting for him. For everyone had heard of his great deeds.

"You have kept your word," said King Arthur. "You have returned in exactly a year and a day. And you have proved yourself. All the land knows of your courage. And of your kindness too. Now you are ready to take your place at the Round Table." King Arthur pointed to the seat beside him.

"Thank you," Sir Lancelot said. He looked at all the knights. "I am proud to be one of you."

King Arthur said, "You are not one of us." He raised his golden cup. "You are the greatest of us all!"

· 3 ·

The Beautiful Witch

One day Merlin came to King Arthur. "I must leave you now," he said. He looked at Arthur with his silvery eyes.

"But why?" King Arthur cried.

"I know my future," Merlin answered quietly. "Soon a fairy maiden will lead me to a great tree. Under its roots will be a cave. I will go inside and fall asleep. With her magic, the fairy will lock me in that cave. And I will stay there."

"But how long must you stay?" King Arthur asked.

"Perhaps forever. Perhaps only until England calls me again."

"How can I be king without you at my side?" King Arthur cried.

"I have taught you all I can," Merlin said. "Just remember. Do not give your trust too easily. What is beautiful is not always good. Fire is warm and bright. But its flames destroy. Be on your guard. Now good-bye, Arthur." Then Merlin was gone. Only a swirl of golden mist remained.

Tears filled Arthur's eyes. How he would miss Merlin!

A few days later King Arthur had a visitor. It was his half sister, Morgan Le Fay. She had ridden to the castle with two of her ladies.

Arthur had not known Morgan until after he became king. She was very beautiful. She had green eyes and hair the color of fire. Arthur loved her dearly.

"My brother," she said, "I was so sorry to hear of Merlin's leaving. I thought you might want me near. A king has so many enemies."

"I thank you," Arthur said. "But I am not afraid. I have my knights. And my magic sword."

"Your sword!" Morgan said. "I have often wished to see it."

King Arthur pulled his sword from the jeweled belt that held it. "My sword is called Excalibur. It bites through armor. It strikes almost with a will of its own." He pointed to the sword belt. "This belt is magic too. Whoever wears it will lose no blood. No matter how badly he is wounded. Merlin told me it would save my life many times."

"A true wonder," Morgan said. "But with Merlin gone, you must be careful. You must guard the sword. Why not leave it with me? No one will guess I have it. I will keep it safe."

"You are right," King Arthur said. "Merlin told me to be on my guard." He put the sword in the magic belt. Then he gave it to her.

As Morgan left she smiled to herself. King Arthur did not know it, but she was a witch. She pretended to love her brother. But she hated him. She was jealous of his power. She meant to take his kingdom for herself. Now she had his sword. And she was going to catch Arthur in a magic trap!

That afternoon King Arthur went hunting deep in the forest. Some of his knights were with him. Morgan was in the forest too. But no one knew it. She had taken the shape of a beautiful white deer.

"Look!" King Arthur pointed through the trees. "A deer as white as snow!" He rode after it. Deeper and deeper into the forest. Only one knight kept up with him. His name was Sir Accolon. He was one of the strongest knights of the Round Table.

The two men rode faster and faster. The deer seemed to be leading them somewhere. It turned and looked around at them. Then, all at once, it disappeared into thin air. King Arthur stopped. They were at the edge of a lake.

Suddenly a golden ship came out of the mist. Its red silk sails were bright as flames. No one seemed to be on the ship.

The ship sailed right onto the shore. As if it were inviting them aboard. "An adventure!" Arthur cried. "Let us visit this strange ship!"

Sir Accolon followed King Arthur. As soon as their feet touched the deck, the ship sailed away on the lake.

Morgan watched from the shore. She was in her own shape now. A wicked smile was on her lips. Arthur had fallen into her trap. If all went well he would soon die. By his own sword. And no one would know she was to blame.

The ship sailed farther and farther on the lake. Darkness fell quickly. Torches suddenly flamed. And twelve lovely maidens appeared. They led King Arthur and Sir Accolon to a table set with wonderful food. The two men ate their fill. They lay on silken pillows. Music played. The smell of flowers filled the air. They fell asleep.

When Arthur awoke, he was lying on a stone floor. It was very dark. The air was damp and cold. He was not on the ship. He was in a dungeon!

A door opened. Light flooded the room. Then a maiden with a torch stood before him. "I come from the lord of the castle," she said. "If you want your freedom, you must fight for it. To the death."

"But I have no sword or armor," Arthur said.

"All you need will be given to you."

"Then I will fight," Arthur said. He looked closely at the maiden. "I think I have seen you before. Have you ever been to my castle?"

"No, never," the maiden said. But she was lying. She had been there. She had come with Morgan Le Fay.

The door clanged shut.

Arthur was afraid. Some evil magic had brought him to this place. Where was the ship? And where was Accolon?

Arthur did not know it, but Accolon was close by. He was lying in a court-yard asleep. A dwarf was watching him. The dwarf's face looked kind. But he was wicked. Morgan Le Fay had sent him to trick Accolon!

Accolon's eyes opened slowly. He

sat up and stared about him in surprise.

"Sir Accolon!" the dwarf said. "I come from King Arthur. He asks you to fight an evil knight. And kill him!" He handed Accolon something wrapped in a silver cloth. "King Arthur has sent you his magic sword."

Accolon unwrapped it carefully. "The king's own sword!" he said. "I must not fail."

The dwarf turned away to hide a wicked smile.

A crowd gathered as King Arthur and Sir Accolon were led to the battlefield. Both men wore strange armor. Both had their helmets closed. Neither guessed who the other really was.

The two men drew their swords. They rushed at each other. They struck again and again.

Accolon had the magic sword. Arthur felt it bite into his armor. Arthur's blood ran down. But no matter how hard Arthur struck, the other knight was never hurt. Accolon was wearing the magic belt. So he lost not a drop of blood.

Suddenly Arthur guessed the truth. He had been tricked! His own magic sword was striking him! Arthur was filled with anger. His anger made him

strong. With a mighty blow, he knocked the magic sword from Accolon's hand. He snatched it up. Then he cut the magic belt from Accolon's waist. Now the other knight had no chance. Arthur struck blow after blow. He knocked Accolon to the ground.

"How did you get this magic sword?" Arthur cried out.

"From King Arthur."

"What!" Arthur cried. He kneeled and took off the knight's helmet. He looked down in horror. It was his friend. Accolon!

Then Arthur took off his own helmet. Accolon stared at him, amazed. "King Arthur! I did not know it was you . . ." His voice was growing weak. "A dwarf brought me the sword. He tricked me. He said King Arthur wanted me to fight . . ." Accolon could speak no more.

"Accolon! Don't die!" Arthur cried. But Accolon was already dead.

Arthur tried to stand up. He was hurt badly. People came closer. They saw who he was. The king! They carried him from the field.

One of Morgan's ladies had watched the battle. She hurried to tell Morgan what had happened.

Morgan was very angry. King Arthur was alive! He had escaped her trap. But she was not going to give up. Not yet. King Arthur was lying somewhere. Helpless. She would find him. And steal the magic sword again!

She called three of her ladies. The sun was setting as they rode away.

Arthur had been taken to a church where the sick were healed. He was very tired. But he would not rest without his magic sword beside him. He drew the sword from its belt. The belt slid to the floor. He lay down with the sword tight in his hand. He fell into a deep sleep.

At that very moment Morgan knocked on the church door. An old woman looked out. Morgan's face seemed sweet and gentle. "I have come to see my brother, the king," she said.

The old woman led Morgan to King Arthur's room and left her alone. Morgan looked around quickly. Where was the magic sword? Then she saw it in Arthur's hand. She knew she could not take it. King Arthur would wake and kill her.

But the magic belt. It lay on the floor. She slipped it under her cloak. Then she rode off into the night.

Soon after, Arthur woke up. He felt that something was wrong. His sword! No, it was still safe in his hand. Then he remembered the magic belt on the floor. That was it. The belt was gone.

Arthur called to the old woman. "Has anyone been here?"

"Only your sister," she answered.

Morgan! Had she stolen his magic belt? Was his sister his enemy?

King Arthur was very weak. But

he called for a horse and rode into the darkness. To find Morgan Le Fay.

Soon he saw four riders. They were far away. But he knew it was Morgan and her ladies. Arthur rode faster.

He came to the top of a hill. Morgan was in the valley below. He could see her clearly.

She rode to a lake. Great rocks stood along its shore. Suddenly she stopped. King Arthur did not understand. What was she going to do? She threw back

her head and laughed. Then she took
the magic belt from under her cloak.
And tossed it into the dark water!

King Arthur was filled with rage.
He raced down the hill. He would
catch her now! But then Morgan, her
ladies, and their horses began to
change. In an instant they turned to
stone. Four more rocks stood in the
valley!

Arthur could hardly believe what
he saw. He could not reach Morgan

now. But at least he knew the truth. Morgan had given his magic sword to Accolon. She had wanted Accolon to kill him. Slowly he rode back to Camelot.

But Arthur had not heard the last of Morgan Le Fay. A few days later a lady came to him. She held out a robe. It glowed and shimmered with rubies. Rubies as red as fire. It was the richest, most beautiful thing Arthur had ever seen.

The lady said, "I come from Morgan. Your sister begs you to forgive her. Someone put her under a magic spell. That is why she did what she did. She sends this gift to show her love. It is a magic robe. Whoever wears it will feel no pain."

King Arthur wanted the beautiful robe. He wanted to believe that

Morgan was true to him. He reached for it. The rubies seemed to blaze with light. Then he seemed to hear Merlin's voice: "What is beautiful is not always good. . . . Be on your guard."

"First try it on yourself," Arthur told the lady.

"Oh, no," the lady said quickly. "Only the king should wear this robe."

"Put it on now," King Arthur said. And he drew his magic sword.

The woman pulled the robe around her shoulders. The instant it touched her, there was a burst of flame. And where she stood only ashes remained.

Arthur stood silent. How close he had been to death! His sister was a powerful enemy. He had escaped her this time. His kingdom was safe. But what of the dangers that lay ahead?

· 4 ·

Sir Gawain and the Lady Ragnell

Sometimes Arthur wished he were not the king. He watched his knights ride off to find adventure. He longed to seek adventure too. But he could not. Not as King Arthur. For who would dare fight the king?

So one morning King Arthur took off his crown. He dressed as an ordinary knight would. And he rode off all alone.

When night fell he was deep in a strange forest. He was cold and tired. And there was nowhere to rest.

He saw a light shining faintly in the distance. He rode toward it. There on a hill stood a castle of black stone. It had seven towers. From each tower a black flag waved. And all around the castle was a moat full of dark water.

King Arthur blew his hunting horn. Then he shouted, "Let down your drawbridge!"

A voice from inside answered, "Go from this place!"

Arthur was angry. "I am a knight of the Round Table. I am tired and cold. You cannot turn me away."

There was silence. Then the voice said, "I will tell my master. But remember. You heard my warning."

A few minutes later there was a clang and a clatter. The drawbridge was let down.

A very old man led King Arthur to a large hall. A fire burned in a fireplace. On the wall above it hung the biggest axe Arthur had ever seen.

A huge man sat by the fire. He was staring into the flames. Then he turned. And Arthur saw his face. He had a patch over one eye. And a deep scar on one cheek. "I am Sir Malger of the Deadly Axe," he said. "Long have I wished to meet a knight of the Round Table. For I have heard they are the bravest knights of all!"

King Arthur was proud of his knights. "You have heard the truth," he said.

The knight stood. He towered over King Arthur. "But not one of them is a match for me!" he said.

Arthur said without fear, "We will see. I will do battle with sword or spear or any weapon you choose."

"A battle!" The knight laughed. "I can kill you with one blow! I challenge you to a true test of bravery. I will give you my axe. It is sharper and heavier than any in the world. I will let you strike me. But then you must let me strike you."

King Arthur stared at the giant axe. "I will do it."

Sir Malger took the axe from the wall. King Arthur could barely lift it.

Sir Malger kneeled. Then he bent his head and held his hair away from his neck. "Strike your blow!"

With all his strength King Arthur lifted the axe. And brought it down. Off flew Sir Malger's head. It rolled about on the floor.

But then the headless knight got to his feet! He picked up his head and placed it on his neck. He was whole again. As though the blow had never been struck!

"Now," Sir Malger said with an evil smile. "Now it is your turn."

King Arthur had been tricked! But he had given his word. With fear in his heart the king kneeled and bent his head. "Strike!" he said. Sir Malger swung the axe high. Arthur closed his eyes. He waited for the blow to fall. But it did not come. He looked up.

"You are a brave man," Sir Malger said. "Perhaps you are wise, too. I will make a bargain with you. I will ask you a riddle. You will have seven days to find the answer. If your answer is right, you can live. If not, you will kneel again for my blow. And this time I will strike! Do you swear to return?"

"Yes," King Arthur said.

"Then here is the riddle. . . . What

is it that women most want? Now go!"

King Arthur left the hall. His heart was beating hard. He rode back into the forest. When he could ride no more, he slept on the cold ground.

He awoke to find one of his bravest knights leaning over him. It was Sir Gawain.

"King Arthur!" he said. "Why are you here?"

Arthur told him all that had happened. When he had finished, Sir Gawain said, "I will go with you. Somehow we will find the answer to the riddle."

For seven days King Arthur and Sir Gawain rode through the land. They asked the riddle of every woman they met. Young maidens with flowers in their hair. Mothers carrying their babies. Poor women tending sheep by the road. Rich ladies covered with jewels.

Some said that women wanted beauty. Some said love. Or wisdom. Or children. Or riches. Or adventure. Or truth. King Arthur remembered all their answers. But somehow he knew that none was right.

On the seventh day Arthur and Gawain rode slowly toward the black castle of Sir Malger. Neither spoke a word.

Suddenly they heard a strange cackle. An old woman was sitting on a log. Her back was to them. She turned and cackled again. King Arthur gasped. Sir Gawain turned pale and looked away.

The old woman was a monster. Her skin was wrinkled and yellow. Her hands were like claws. She had only

a few jagged teeth and a patch over one eye.

She looked at King Arthur and cackled again. "You will go to your death, King Arthur!" she screeched. "Unless I help you!"

The two men looked at each other.

"Oh, yes," the woman went on. "I know the answer to the riddle. The only answer that will save your life. And I will tell you, if you make me a promise."

King Arthur felt a stir of hope. "What is it that you wish, my lady?"

"I am Lady Ragnell." She smiled at Arthur. He tried not to shiver at the awful sight. "And I want one of your knights as a husband."

"That I cannot promise!"

Sir Gawain stared at Lady Ragnell. He had never seen such a horrible creature. But he said. "If the answer can save my king's life, I will marry this lady."

"I cannot let you do that," Arthur said quietly.

"You must. We cannot lose our king."

Arthur knew that Gawain was right. So at last he said to the old woman, "Tell me the answer."

Lady Ragnell called him over and whispered in his ear.

King Arthur almost smiled at her words. Could this be the answer Sir Malger wanted? Perhaps it *was* what women wanted most. And men as well.

He mounted his horse.

"In two days' time I will be at Camelot," Lady Ragnell called. "For my wedding!" She laughed again. There was nothing happy in the sound.

When the two men reached the edge of the forest, King Arthur told Gawain to wait. "I must go alone," he said.

He rode up the hill. There was the dark castle. Sir Malger stood on the drawbridge. He was sharpening the giant axe.

"You keep your promises," he said to Arthur. He held up his axe. "And I keep mine. Now. What is your answer? What do women want most?"

Then Arthur repeated the many answers he had heard.

"No, no," Malger said. He lifted his axe. "Bend your head. It is time."

"Wait," King Arthur said. "I have one more answer. I learned it from an old woman in the forest. What women want most is to have their own way!"

Malger roared with anger. "My sister! Lady Ragnell! She told you. She has cheated me. But I keep my word. You may live! But do not pass this way again!"

King Arthur rode off. He was free. But he was not happy. Gawain was going to pay a terrible price for Arthur's life.

Two days later Sir Gawain and Lady Ragnell were married. No one was asked to the wedding. No one except King Arthur.

But Gawain was loved by all. His friends didn't understand why no one was there. So they prepared a wedding feast in the Great Hall. And everyone waited to wish Gawain happiness.

Someone cried, "They are coming!" The knights and ladies began to cheer. Then Gawain and his bride walked into the hall. And the cheers died away.

Lady Ragnell was dressed in a beautiful gown. But nothing could hide her terrible face. Gawain was pale. But he held his head high.

For a moment not a sound could be heard. But Lancelot was always kind. And someone had to greet the bride. He tried to keep the horror from his voice. "Welcome, my lady. Good wishes to you and our dear friend Gawain."

Then everyone began to talk brightly and laugh loudly. They pretended to be happy. This was a wedding after all! But they kept their eyes away from Lady Ragnell.

Finally the feast was over. Sir Gawain sat at the table alone. Everyone had said good night. And Lady Ragnell had gone off to their tower room.

Gawain wished he could saddle his horse and ride away. Forever. But he was a knight of the Round Table. And he had made a promise. So he had to hide his feelings. He had to try to be a good husband.

He climbed the stairs to the tower. Slowly he opened the door. A log glowed in the fireplace. But the room was dark. For a moment he thought Lady Ragnell was gone! Then the flames glowed more brightly. He saw her sitting in a chair by the fire. How horrible she was.

"Greetings, husband! Come, give me a kiss!"

Gawain thought of his promise. He tried to smile at his wife. He closed his eyes. And kissed her gently.

Then a sweet, soft voice said, "Thank you, my Gawain."

He opened his eyes. And there was a beautiful woman! Gawain stepped back. He was amazed. "Who are you? Where is Lady Ragnell?"

The woman held out her arms. Her face was full of love. "I am Lady Ragnell."

Sir Gawain just stared.

The woman smiled gently. "This

is my true self. Sir Malger put me under an evil spell. Because you were so good and kind, I am partly free now. But only partly. For half of each day I will look as I do now. But for the other half, I will look as horrible as before."

She took Gawain's hand. "So you must choose. And it is a hard choice. I can take my own shape in the night or in the day. Which shall it be? Think

carefully. If I am a monster by day, you will be shamed before all the world. But if I am a monster at night, you will not be happy in your own home."

Sir Gawain looked into her eyes. "You are the one who must bear this burden. You must choose. Not I."

"Gawain!" Lady Ragnell's face was shining with joy. "Do you remember the riddle? You have let me choose. You have given me what all women want. My own way. Now you have broken the spell forever! I need never take that monster shape again. I can be my true self. Day, night, and always!"

Gawain had never felt such joy. And the next day he gave another wedding feast for his bride. It was the happiest ever seen at Camelot.

· 5 ·

The Kitchen Knight

Once each year all the knights of the Round Table met for a special feast. The Round Table was set with wonderful foods. There were loaves of bread. Steaming roasts. Goblets of wine. Fruits and honey cakes.

King Arthur and his knights sat at the table. They laughed and joked. But no one sipped his wine or tasted his bread. For on this special day King Arthur had a rule. The feast would not begin until a stranger came before them. With a wonderful story to tell. A question to ask. Or an adventure to offer.

On one such feast day Sir Gawain stood at the window. "We will eat soon," he called. "I see a man coming. He is as handsome as a prince. And almost as tall as a giant!"

The door to the Great Hall swung open. There stood a tall young man. He came into the Great Hall.

"Who are you?" Arthur asked kindly. "And why do you come here?"

The young man spoke softly. "I cannot tell my name. But I wish to ask for three gifts. I will ask for one now. The others a year from this day."

"You will have whatever you ask," Arthur told him. "As long as it will not hurt anyone. And it is in my power to give."

"Then for one year I want food to eat at your castle," the young man said.

Food! Everyone was surprised. Most of them decided the young man was just a beggar.

King Arthur looked closely at the stranger. "Are you sure that is all you want?"

"Only that," the young man answered.

"Then go with Sir Kay. He is the keeper of my castle. Kay, give this young man food fit for a lord."

"I will stuff this lazy fellow until he is as fat as a hog!" Kay said with a loud laugh. "He can stay in the kitchen. Right next to the stewpot! But he needs a name. Since he's ashamed to tell his own!"

Gawain liked something about the young man. "Go easy with the boy, Kay."

Lancelot spoke up too. "You know nothing about this stranger. You need not be mean."

Kay looked the young man up and down. "I have it! Look at those great big white hands. He must think they are much too fine for work. His name will be Big Hands!"

And that is what everyone called him.

All year long Big Hands worked in

the kitchen. Lancelot and Gawain were kind to him. They smiled and joked with him. They gave him coins to spend. But Kay poked fun at him all the time. He gave him the dirtiest jobs to do. Still, Big Hands was always quiet and polite.

A year went by. And again the day of the great feast came. Again King Arthur and his knights sat at the Round Table. And again they waited for a stranger.

This time a lovely maiden came into the hall. She kneeled before King Arthur. "You must help me!" she cried. "I am Lady Linnet. My sister, Linness, is kept prisoner in her own castle. By the terrible Red Knight of the Red Lawns. Please give me a brave knight to set her free!"

Sir Gawain said, "The Red Knight

has the strength of seven men. He has magic powers. He grows stronger and stronger as the sun rises in the sky. Only at sunset does his strength fade. Dozens of knights have died fighting him."

Suddenly Big Hands' voice rang out. "King Arthur! For a year I have worked in your kitchen. I ask now for the other gifts you promised me." He was standing very straight. His eyes were shining.

"Go back to your pots and pans," Kay called. And there was laughter.

Big Hands paid no attention. "First, let me go on this adventure. Let Sir Lancelot follow after me. Then, when I prove myself, let him make me a knight."

"Gladly," said the king.

Lady Linnet was pale with anger.

"The best knights in the world are here. Sir Lancelot! Sir Gawain! And you give me your kitchen boy!" She left the Great Hall and rode away.

Big Hands had no armor, no sword, and no shield. But he grabbed a spear and rode after her.

Linnet was far from Camelot by the time Big Hands caught up to her.

She was still angry. "Go away!" she cried. "You stink of the kitchen!"

Big Hands answered her politely. "Lady Linnet, I have promised the king. I will free your sister. Or I will die trying."

Linnet laughed. "Brave words for a pot-washer! But you will not get far. This path is full of danger. Just look!"

There in a clearing was a knight. His armor was black. He had a black horse. And he carried a black spear and shield.

"That is the Black Knight of the Black Lawns," said Linnet. "He is the brother of the Red Knight. The knight who keeps my sister prisoner. The Black Knight lets no one pass this way. You had best run back to your brooms and mops!"

Big Hands said only, "We shall see, my lady."

Then the Black Knight called in a

voice like thunder, "Turn back or die!"

Big Hands shouted, "I will pass. Stop me if you can!"

The two men rode toward each other as fast as their horses could carry them. The Black Knight's spear only brushed against Big Hands. But Big Hands' blow was hard and true. The Black Knight fell to the ground.

Big Hands leaped from his horse. In an instant he had his spear at the Black Knight's heart.

"Let me live!" the Black Knight cried. "I have thirty knights. They will be yours to command."

"Swear that you will fight only for what is good and true," Big Hands told him. "Go with your men to King Arthur. And say you were sent by the knight with no name."

The Black Knight gave his word.

Then Big Hands looked for Lady Linnet. She was gone! He took the Black Knight's sword and shield and helmet. What did she think of his fight with the Black Knight?

He soon had his answer. He rode up beside her. She said, "I knew you must be near. I smelled grease and garbage. I saw you fight the Black Knight. But do not expect me to think better of you. I was not fooled. The sun was in the Black Knight's eyes. Or you would be lying in the dust."

Big Hands tried not to show his anger. He answered, "Your words do not please me. But I still mean to free your sister from the Red Knight."

"Soon you will wish for your kitchen," Lady Linnet told him. "Much more danger lies before us."

The next day they came to a river.

There was only one place to cross. But a knight on horseback barred the way. He was bigger than the Black Knight. His spear and shield were green. He wore green armor. It seemed to gleam with a blinding light.

"That is the Green Knight of the Green Lawns," said Lady Linnet. "Run, kitchen boy. Or you will die!"

"I will do my best to live." And Big Hands lowered his spear.

The Green Knight was strong. But Big Hands was stronger still. He aimed his spear and sent the Green Knight crashing to the ground. Before the Green Knight could move, Big Hands stood over him. "Spare my life!" the Green Knight cried.

"Only if this lady asks it," Big Hands answered.

"I ask no favors of a kitchen boy!"

Linnet cried. The Green Knight moaned. So she said to Big Hands, "Oh, very well. Let the knight go. But I think no better of you. His horse must have stumbled. Or you would be lying in the mud."

Big Hands made the Green Knight promise to give himself up to King Arthur. Then he helped the knight to his feet. The Green Knight frowned at Linnet. "My lady, I have fought many men. But none can match this one. He does not deserve your words."

"You must like the stink of the kitchen too!" Linnet said, and rode off.

Big Hands sighed. But he kept following after Linnet.

Big Hands fought many more battles. He beat the Blue Knight. And the Brown Knight. Yet still Linnet called him names. She made excuses for the fallen knights. "His spear was broken," she would say. Or "His saddle was loose." "The Red Knight is a hundred times more deadly," Linnet kept telling Big Hands. "You will never beat him."

Finally Big Hands saw a castle. Around it were many red tents. And hundreds of soldiers all in red too.

"We are here," Linnet said.

They rode closer. Big Hands saw a huge oak tree. Many shields hung from it. They were of different colors and designs. A great silver horn hung there too.

"Those shields belonged to the men the Red Knight killed," Linnet said. "He hung them as a warning. Anyone who wishes to fight must blow the silver horn. Then he will come."

Big Hands reached for the horn.

"No, not yet!" Linnet cried. "The Red Knight is at his strongest now. Wait. As the sun sinks in the sky he will grow weaker."

Big Hands stared at her. "Why do you think me such a coward! To fight a man when he is weakest? That would be shameful!"

And Big Hands blew the horn.

A woman came to the castle window. Big Hands stared. She was beautiful! "That is my sister!" cried Linnet.

Big Hands sounded the horn again. This time he saw a cloud of dust. A huge knight was galloping toward him. He was the largest man Big Hands had ever seen. His armor was the color of blood. It seemed to blaze and burn in the sunlight.

He was the Red Knight!

For a moment Big Hands could not speak or move. Then he called, "Free the lady Linness! Or die!"

The Red Knight did not answer. He laughed a terrible laugh. And then he lowered his spear.

The two men rode toward each other. The ground shook with the weight of their horses. Spear crashed against shield. Both horses fell. Both spears broke. And both men lay on the ground. They were as still as death.

The Red Knight stirred. Lady Linnet gasped. Then Big Hands moved too. Both men took up their swords. They came at each other again. Soon the ground was dark with blood.

Big Hands fell to his knees. The Red Knight lifted his sword high. But Big Hands twisted away. He rushed at the Red Knight. He ran his sword through the Red Knight's heart.

The Red Knight lay dead.

Big Hands turned to Lady Linnet. She did not thank him. She did not say she was sorry for her cruel words. She said, "What luck!"

And then she smiled. But not at Big Hands. A beautiful woman was walking toward them. The woman at the window. The lady Linness.

Big Hands caught his breath. He had never seen such a lovely face.

"My dear sister!" Linnet cried. And the two women threw their arms around each other.

Then Linness turned to Big Hands. "Sir Knight," she said, "how can I thank you?"

"There is no need," Linnet said. "He is only a kitchen boy."

Linness gasped. "For shame, Linnet! This is the bravest man I have ever seen!" She looked at Big Hands. "I vowed to marry the man who freed me. If you wish, I am yours."

Big Hands tried to read her face. "I loved you the moment I saw you. But would you truly marry a kitchen boy?"

Linness smiled up at him. "I would be proud to have you as my husband."

At that moment a knight came riding across the field. It was Sir Lancelot! He had been watching Big Hands from the moment he left Arthur's castle.

"You have earned your knighthood many times over," Lancelot told Big Hands. "I will make you a knight. Then we will return to Camelot. What a surprise we will give everyone!"

A few days later King Arthur was

sitting in the Great Hall. Many of his knights and ladies were there too.

Sir Gawain stood by the window. Suddenly he called, "What a strange sight! Here is a whole army of men. I see a knight in black. And one in green. One in blue. And one in brown. They are all coming to the castle!"

Soon the hall was crowded. All the knights Big Hands had fought were there. And their followers too. Each man promised to be loyal to King Arthur from then on. Each said that the knight with no name had sent him.

Everyone was amazed. Who could this wonderful knight be?

Then there was a loud knocking at the door.

Sir Lancelot walked in. With him were Linness and Linnet. And a knight in full armor. His face was hidden by his helmet. Lancelot said, "I bring the man who did these great deeds."

The knight took off his helmet.

There was a gasp of surprise. It was Big Hands. The kitchen boy.

Everyone began to laugh. Was this a joke?

But King Arthur said, "Bravely done! Will you now tell us who you are?"

Big Hands smiled at Linness. Then he looked at Linnet. He had a twinkle in his eye. "I am the son of a king."

Linnet turned bright red. The

kitchen boy was really a prince! For once she had nothing to say.

Big Hands went on. "I have an older brother. I love him very much. He left our country when I was but a child. He joined the Round Table. He did not know me when I came. But perhaps he will now." He smiled at Sir Gawain. "My name is Gareth."

Sir Gawain pushed through the crowd. Tears were in his eyes. He threw his arms around his brother. "My dear Gareth! Why did you hide who you were? I would have made the way easy for you."

"That is why." Gareth smiled. "I wanted to make my own way. To win my own place."

"And it is a place of great honor," King Arthur said. "Welcome, Sir Gareth, knight of the Round Table!"

· 6 ·

The Last Battle

The fame of the Round Table spread far and wide. King Arthur's knights rode through the land. They helped the poor and the weak. Wherever they found evil, they fought against it. Brave men came from many countries to join the Round Table. And gold letters spelled their names upon their chairs.

But the years passed. King Arthur's hair turned silver. His knights, too, grew older. Some died. Some returned to the homes they had left long ago.

Now there were empty places at the Round Table. And no gold letters wrote the names of new knights to come. King Arthur knew the glory of the Round Table was near its end.

Then an evil knight came to Camelot. His name was Sir Mordred. And

he was the son of Morgan Le Fay. Mordred pretended to love King Arthur. But like his mother before him, he wanted the throne for himself.

Mordred went secretly to the new knights of the Round Table. He laughed at King Arthur and his promises. "Help the weak!" he said. "How foolish! Let us fight for ourselves. Let us take what we want. Land. Gold. The kingdom itself!" The knights listened to Mordred. He gathered more and more men around him. They were ready to fight King Arthur.

But some knights were still true to Arthur. He called them all together. "This is the greatest danger our land has ever faced. Our numbers are few. Many of our strongest knights are gone. Lancelot is in his home across the sea. Gawain is dead. Still we must stop Mordred."

Arthur and his knights rode out to fight Sir Mordred. They stopped at nightfall. The battle would be the next day. That night Arthur sat staring into his campfire. He began to doze.

All at once Arthur saw Gawain's face. And he heard Gawain's voice. "Do not fight now," Gawain said. "Or you will die. The rule of right and good will end. Promise Mordred anything. But do not fight. Lancelot will come to help. In one month he will be here and all will be saved." And then Gawain's voice faded away.

Arthur shook himself. Was it a dream? Or had Gawain's ghost come to warn him?

Arthur called one of his best knights. Sir Bedivere. "Go and make peace with Mordred," Arthur told him. "Give him what you must. We need time."

Bedivere went. Mordred agreed not to fight. As long as King Arthur promised him the rule of half the kingdom. And all the rest when Arthur died.

The next morning Arthur and Mordred each set off to meet together and make the peace. But King Arthur did not trust Mordred. He told his men, "Be on your guard. If one sword is drawn, we will fight."

Mordred did not trust King Arthur either. He warned his men, "If anyone draws a sword, kill them all."

The two armies were face to face as the sun rose. Arthur and Mordred rode up to each other. Ready to make the peace. Arthur could hardly bear to look at Mordred's proud, evil face. But he wanted peace. For then perhaps the Round Table would not end.

Just then a snake slithered through the grass. It bit one of King Arthur's knights. The knight did not think. He drew his sword. He cut the snake in two.

Mordred's men saw the flash of the sword. And in an instant the battle had begun.

The armies galloped toward each other. Arrows filled the air. Spears crashed against shields. Brave knights fell. Others were wounded. Blood stained the earth. But both sides fought on.

It was almost dark. The battlefield grew quiet. King Arthur looked around him. Of all his knights only two were alive. And they were wounded. Sir Lucan and Sir Bedivere.

Tears ran down King Arthur's face. Just then he saw someone else still standing. Mordred!

"Give me my spear!" Arthur cried. He ran toward his enemy. "You will not do more evil!" he shouted. Mordred saw him. Arthur sank his spear deep into Mordred's heart. But as he died Mordred swung his sword one last time. Arthur fell with a terrible wound.

Sir Bedivere went to him. Arthur opened his eyes. He pointed to a lake nearby. Then he told Bedivere, "My time has come. Take my magic sword and throw it in the lake. And tell me what you see."

Sir Bedivere took the beautiful

sword. But he thought to himself, "How can I throw away the king's sword?" And he hid it under the roots of a tree.

When he came back, King Arthur asked, "Tell me, what did you see?"

Bedivere answered, "Nothing but the moon on the water."

Then Arthur told him, "You have not done what I asked. Go back. And hurry!"

Bedivere went back to the tree. He took the sword in his hand. But still he thought, "I cannot bear to throw my dear king's sword away." So he left it.

When he returned, Arthur asked again, "Tell me what you saw."

And Bedivere said, "Nothing but the wind in the trees."

This time King Arthur said, "You

have been false to me again! It grows late. My life is leaving me. I can wait no longer. Now, if you care for me, do as I say!"

Then Sir Bedivere was sorry. He found the sword. And he took it to the water's edge. He threw it into the lake as far and as hard as he could.

The sword gleamed in the moonlight. Then a hand rose out of the water. It caught the sword. And disappeared beneath the waves.

Bedivere told King Arthur what he had seen. Arthur nodded. "Now help me to the water's edge. And hurry. I have so little time. I am afraid I have waited too long."

When they reached the shore, a boat was there. Three women were in it. They wore crowns and long black veils. When they saw King Arthur, they began to cry softly.

"Put me in the boat," Arthur said. Sir Bedivere set him down gently. One of the women cried, "Oh, Arthur! Why did you wait so long? Your wound has grown cold."

The boat sailed slowly into the mist. Sir Bedivere called out, "My king! Will you return?"

King Arthur answered, "I am going to a magic land. There I will be healed. Unless it is too late. But if England

has need of me, I will come again."
And the boat disappeared in the mist.

Some say King Arthur died. Some say he is sleeping an enchanted sleep. Some say he lives on in a land of mists and magic. And that one day he will return. And there will be a new kingdom of the good and the true.